# Driven to Death

## Marty M. Engle

P9-ELR-963

A
MONTAGE
PUBLICATION

22,888

Montage Publications, a Front Line company,
San Diego, California

ISBN 1-56714-038-6

Printed in the U.S.A.

**TO OUR FAMILIES
&
FRIENDS**
*(You know who you are.)*

The tops of the masts rose high in the glass case. The sails, made of real cloth and tied with real string, hung low, crisscrossed with plastic rigging.

The captain's wheel could actually turn, moving the rudder with it.

The removable cannons pointed out from windows cut in the rounded plastic sides.

I remembered painting each piece of trim and gluing each crate to the deck.

I peered through one of the windows and saw the tiny skeleton chained to a wall in the brig, even tinier plastic rats glued all around him.

"That took forever to get right," I said to myself as I stepped back from the old masterpiece gathering dust in my garage.

My name is Darren Donaldson. I am thirteen years old and I love building models. I have been building models for three years now and have become very good at it. Dad says I have a real talent.

The garage held quite a collection. A beautiful eighteen wheeler truck with a trailer and working lights (it gave me nothing but trouble and took two weeks to put together). A nuclear submarine nearly three feet long. A bunch of ships from Star Wars, and my crowning achievment; the crown jewel in my collection and a source of admiration from all my peers.

A pirate ship.

The moonlight, shining through the dust of the tiny windows in the garage door, would light up the sails and take your breath away.

At Fairfield Junior High it is widely regarded as the most beautiful model ever assembled. Painted in every detail; dry-brushed wooden planks to make it look old; small rips in the sails; spray-painted smoke stains around every opened cannon window.

I read about a dozen books on pirates

before I started, to be sure of every detail.

Dad put it in a glass case for me on the day I moved it to the garage from my room.

That became the saddest day of my life for two reasons.

One, it meant I had to start looking for other places to store my models or get rid of some old ones. Something I couldn't even think about and. . .

Two, it was the first time my older brother David didn't help me finish a model.

David always helped me put the finishing touches on my models and never took any credit for it. We always had a great time, painting and sanding and detailing. He would be the first to brag about my attention to detail and painting expertise.

But this time he barely acknowledged my existence. He seemed mopy and sad and wanted to be left alone. We hardly did anything together anymore.

Except on Thursday movie night. Dad would make us both go to the video store with him and the whole family would watch whatever we rented. I love watching movies almost as much as building models, especially scary ones.

The one thing David and I agree on is the type of movies we rent. What else? Horror movies!

Mom hates it when we rent horror movies, but Dad lets us get away with it, if it's not too scary.

Anyway, I walked over to the car and waited. The garage lights were off. The moonlight streamed in through the windows, striking the sails of the ship and filling them with light. I could have watched it for hours.

Then David turned the lights on.

"Shotgun," he muttered.

His bad mood practically oozed out.

"No way! I was here way before you. I get the front!" Rules are rules, after all.

"Shotgun," David said again as he jumped in the driver's side and slid over, locking the front door.

I puffed up, ready to clobber him when I heard Dad coming down the stairs to the garage. I am not very tall, but I'm stocky and I love a good fight, especially with David.

"NO SCARY MOVIES!" Mom yelled

down the stairs as Dad popped into sight, keys in hand.

"Ready to go, guys?"

Dad loves movie night almost as much as I do.

"You bet, Dad." I slapped David's window as I hopped in the backseat. I wouldn't let the grump king of the universe ruin my movie night.

The grump king grumbled and sulked in his seat as the car started.

"C'mon David. Give it up. I am not letting you hang out at McDonald's parking lot all hours of the night. Friends or no friends. It won't kill you to spend a little time with your family."

"YEAH! Tell him, Dad!"

David let his seat fall back and hit me in the head. His smile filled the rear view mirror.

"Get off, moron!" I shoved the seat back up and flipped the back of his ear.

"Enough, Darren," Dad said. "I promised your mother we would get back quick. David, are you going to be a spoil sport all night?"

"No," David sighed. He didn't fool either

of us. He would be the grump king until we got there, then he would snap out of it. Same thing happened every Thursday.

Until now.

Our video store is in a busy shopping center near our house. It's the only place to hang out after school and at night. It has a McDonald's and a video store and a grocery store. On the upper level is a music store and a comic shop. All this within walking distance of our house. I practically lived there.

"Darren, we're almost there. Get down!" my brother called from the front seat, as he ducked out of view.

I slid down in my seat as low as I could. The red and yellow wash of light from the McDonald's sign crawled across the seat.

"You guys sit up! This is ridiculous," Dad snapped.

"No way, Dad. You know the deal," David protested.

From the windows and parking lot of McDonald's, it would appear as if the blue Toyota Celica cruising toward the video store contained only its middle-aged driver. David and I simply couldn't afford to be seen.

McDonald's was the spot to hang out with your friends. Guys would make the loop there and drive up and down the main street, come back down to McDonald's and make the loop again. Everyone would stop out in the parking lot to change cars and meet girls and occasionally even buy food. It was *the* place.

David loved hanging out there as much as he could. Unfortunately, Dad wouldn't let him drive that much because he just got his license.

He couldn't hang out without a car. It simply wasn't done. And no one allowed themselves to be *dropped off*.

Dad didn't care. He drove us right by our peers, unknowing and uncaring of the horrible social ramifications of such a scene.

"Okay, okay. You can sit up now. No one will see you with your horrible, leper father." Dad sounded half-kidding, half-upset.

David let me know when the coast was

clear. "Okay, Darren. It's cool." He jerked back up into his seat.

I popped back up and gave Dad a good old fashioned choke hold around the throat. Not hard or anything. Just playing.

"HEY! All right. All right. Settle down, Darren," Dad laughed.

He got on David and me for playing too rough. We never really hurt each other. David actually sticks up for me. If somebody picks on me or threatens me, David's there. Despite his moodiness, he's okay for a big brother. He's just grumpy by nature.

Dad pulled into a spot in front of the video store and looked around, exaggerating every turn of his head. He smiled and winked at me.

"Well, would it permanently scar your reputation if you're seen in a public video store with your old man?"

He nudged David who softened slightly and even smiled.

"I'll live."

"All right."

David and Dad high-fived. As always.

David made it across the store and half way down the horror aisle by the time Dad's hand left my shoulder. "Remember what your mother said, Darren. Nothing scary."

Yeah, right. Every Thursday, the same thing. Nothing scary meant get one horror movie, not three.

Like I said before, Mom and Dad are pretty cool about letting us watch horror movies. As long as they aren't rated R. Of course this cut the number of horror movies we could see in half, but half's better than nothing.

"YES! cool. This is the one, Darren!" David called out down the aisle. I ran over to see what he grabbed off the shelf. It was the same movie he picked last time.

"Not again, David. Let's get something different," I whined, not anxious to see "Duel" again. It's a cool movie, but I've seen it so many times I can recite the whole thing.

It's about this guy and a giant truck that tries to run him down in the desert. The cool thing about it is, you never see the driver. Only his ugly hairy arm hanging out the window. I painted my truck model to look like the one in the movie.

"No way. Get what you want. I'm getting this one." David grabbed the bright blue box off the shelf.

"Come on, David. You know we can only get one horror movie. I don't want to see that one again. Let's get something new."

"Here comes Dad. We're getting this one!" David the grump king smugly shook the box in front of me. . . then stopped.

Suddenly David's eyes got as big as two saucers. All the boxes in the aisle had started shaking, a hundred boxes!

They began to fly off the shelves!

One by one!

Neither David nor I said a word as the boxes flew around, one after another in a wave, as if some unseen giant arm knocked them off as it went by. It headed straight down the aisle toward us!

I looked at David, who could only stare as the avalanche of boxes suddenly stopped.

Every shelf in the entire horror section stood empty. We stood in the knee high boxes strewn on the floor.

I heard a horrible high-pitched chuckle, like a rotten little kid's laugh, as people from all over the store rushed over.

"What did you guys do!?" Dad demanded. The manager stood beside Dad and both turned the same angry shade of red.

The next thing I knew, David and I

found ourselves sitting in the car, staring blankly at the front window of the video store.

At that moment, our father was picking up boxes with the video store manager.

"We didn't do anything, David!" I cried.

"Just shut up, Darren."

"Maybe it was some spastic creep on the other side of the aisle! Or a small earthquake!"

"The size of a video aisle? That's a real small quake, lamebrain."

"Don't get mad at me. I didn't do anything. It's not my fault." Too late. The grump king sat on his throne in full pout.

"Just shut up, okay?" David said again, only louder and nastier. I smacked him on the back of the head. He jumped over the seat and we started fighting in the back.

Suddenly a set of headlights appeared on the frontage road behind us, cruising toward the McDonald's.

If we hadn't been fighting, maybe I would have seen the lights sooner.

They came from a strange cruising car that made no noise, but moved swiftly and silently with no help from an engine

. . . and no driver

At first I didn't notice the three guys huddled in its back seat, staring at me with their horrible faces and weird, unearthly grins.

Then I heard the chuckle, the same chuckle that I heard echo in the video aisle.

I stopped fighting and looked out the back window.

The mysterious car vanished in a burst of light. Right before my eyes.

"Did you see that?" I asked David.

"See what?"

"That CAR! That's what. You saw it, too. I know you did. It disappeared. Right in front of us!" I squawked, the full reality of what I'd seen hitting me hard.

"I didn't see anything," David said.

Dad opened the door and flopped the videotape of "Duel", along with two others, on the seat beside us.

"All right, knock it off," Dad said as he closed his door and David climbed back into the front. "I don't know what you two were try-ing to pull in there, but you're both grounded for a week."

"WHAT! Dad, we didn't do anything!" I

yelped, rising up from my seat.

"I suppose all those tapes just flew off the shelves by themselves?" Dad started the car. "You're being grounded for fighting in the car, too."

"Good job, Darren," David cracked.

I smacked him on the back of the head, harder than before.

He turned to retaliate but Dad stopped him. "Enough. Or do you want to try for two weeks? I swear, we can't go anywhere without you two starting something." Dad began to take the turn toward McDonald's.

The crowd at McDonald's had grown. Almost everyone David knew from school was there. Everyone laughed and ran around, getting in different cars.

Neither David nor I ducked down this time. I kept seeing that car vanish in my head, wondering if I had imagined the whole thing.

A couple of David's friends waved at him and honked. David didn't wave back.

Dad waved for him. Ouch.

The grump king would rule for the rest of the evening.

Or so I thought.

A half hour into the movie, David decided he finally had enough of monster trucks, ugly hairy arms and gas pump explosions.

With a sigh, he got up and left the room. He passed Dad, asleep in his chair, and Mom, working on her cross-stitch pattern, lost in her own world of needlework.

Thursday movie night routine. The movie would play until it ended. Mom would turn off the lights and Dad would lock up. David would eat anything he could find in the kitchen and I would go up to bed.

I had settled into bed by the time David came into our room with a loud burp.

I continued to pick off the stack of comic books beside my bed. When I read comics, I go through my whole collection that I keep in four piles in the closet. I decide on four or five different heroes and then pick out a bunch of comics featuring each hero.

I make sure they're all in order, and stack them in the sequence I want to read them. A good two hours or more can be lost.

David saw the stack and shook his head. Before he could say anything, Dad stuck his head in the door.

"Good night, boys. We're going to bed."

"Good night, Dad."

"Night, Dad," I said from behind Daredevil #237. He saw the pile of comics.

"Darren, get to sleep pretty soon." He closed the door.

David cracked the door open and carefully peered down the hall.

He put his jacket on. Odd.

The clock read eleven thirty.

"Hey, Sparky. Where do you think you're going?" I asked.

"I have to get out of here. I'm going nuts," David said, zipping up his jacket.

"You're going to walk all the way up to the McDonald's at this hour?" I asked, shuffling through my stack of comic books, anxious for another.

"I'm not going to walk." David reached for his wallet on the dresser.

Oh, man. Trouble.

"You can't be serious? Dad'll kill you," I said, now alert and on my feet.

"I don't care. I'm going nuts tonight. I'll be back in about an hour." David shoved a couple of cassettes in his pocket.

"McDonald's is closed! Only the drive-thru is open! There isn't anybody up there anymore!"

No use.

He knew there were stragglers hanging out in the parking lot until midnight or even later. He'd done this before.

"Later." David quietly closed the bedroom door behind him.

Man. I hated this. If I told on him, he'd never talk to me again. If he got caught, I'd really catch it from Mom and Dad for not telling on him.

In my mind, I saw David tiptoe through the kitchen, his hand outstretched toward the extra car key Dad keeps on a hook by the coffee maker.

In just a few moments, I would look out the bedroom window and watch David silently push the car onto the street. He would coast about three houses down. Then the lights would come on, the engine would roar to life and he would take off on the ride of the grump king to McDonalds.

I went to the window to watch. Any second now, the tip of the car's rear end would come into view.

There.

A soft crunching sound as the tires slowly rolled across the driveway, the cold blue moonlight reflecting from the hood.

The grump king had gotten away with it again. At least so far.

Three houses down the engine started up, right on cue. I guessed he would drive around for about an hour, listening to his tapes.

I watched as the red tail lights vanished down the street.

*Three hours later, he hadn't come back.*

I sat on my bed, staring out the window. Waiting. Wondering where David could possibly be at 2:30 in the morning. He had never stayed away for so long before.

Oh, man. Any minute now, Mom and Dad would come barreling into the room demanding to know where David went.

I would swear I didn't know.

Dad would say, "I'm going to look for him." He would go to the garage and then... I couldn't even imagine about what would happen next. Any minute now. I knew it.

Around 3:15 in the morning, I decided David met with serious trouble. Half the contents of my comic closet sat on the floor beside my bed. I had all the lights off to keep suspicion away, should Mom or Dad wake up and head to the kitchen.

I had a flashlight on, holding it to my chin and pulling it away. Then I would shine it straight up and hold my hand over it so it would look like a giant claw coming down from the ceiling. To say I was nervous was the understatement of the year.

At 3:30, I put my jacket on, shoved my comics into mini piles under the bed and stared out the window, hoping beyond hope the family car would turn into the driveway.

No such luck.

I decided I would have to go find my idiot brother myself, before he got us both killed.

When he didn't come back after that first hour, I should have told Mom and Dad.

Too late now.

*I* had to go find him or risk permanent grounding . . . or worse.

I sat back on the bed for one more moment. Should I do this? Look at the TIME!

I would be setting myself up for big time trouble if I went looking for him this late. Plus, how far could I get on foot? What if he didn't go to McDonalds? What if he snuck over to a friend's house or something?

No way could I do this! What was I thinking? It's his own stupid fault! I could just go to bed! YEAH!

I could act like I slept through the whole thing. I didn't even know he left! It's his mess. I slept right through it.

Twenty seconds later I jumped into bed.

Then I heard a car coming down our street. No mistake. I could tell by the sound of the engine. Our car. Definitely our car. A wave of relief washed over me.

I ran to the window.

I saw it! The blue Celica. It headed down our street and toward the house. Not from McDonald's, though. He must have gone somewhere else. What a relief! Now if my idiot brother could only sneak the car into the garage.

Three houses down. Two. Wait a minute. He wasn't slowing down. He SPED UP...the car swerving all over the road! He almost hit the Pickerman's mailbox next door!

My head spun and I felt a burst of nausea. Everything in my room started to shake. Trophies vibrated on the shelf. I heard my mini piles of comics topple over under my bed. The window rattled in the frame.

The lights of our car shut off and the engine died. David bolted from the driver's side door and ran behind the car, still a house length away.

I saw him strain against the bumper under the streetlights.

He struggled, pushing the quiet, dead car toward the driveway. He seemed frantic!

I didn't understand! He should be careful! He would wake Mom and Dad!

My blood suddenly froze. He looked straight at me from the street. He mouthed something but I couldn't tell what. He looked scared. Almost terrified.

That's when I saw a second set of headlights rushing down the street.

I ran down the stairs, easing past Mom and Dad's room. Someone was after David. Someone mad. I jumped down the last three steps and ran to the door.

I fumbled with the lock for a moment, then felt the cold night air as the door swung open. David frantically hissed at me to help, desperately shoved the car toward the driveway.

"Darren! Help me! Quick!" David strained, pushing our car in desperation. The headlights from the second car were bearing-down fast, only six houses away.

I cut across the yard, ran behind our car and pushed with all my might. I had a million questions, but they would have to wait.

Together we shoved the car into the driveway. Too fast. It started to get away from us!

"Darren! Get in and steer!" David whispered, grabbing the bumper.

Our sneakers pounded the pavement. The other car roared up behind us! It grazed the mailbox that David missed a few moments earlier.

I clutched the door handle, threw it open, scrambled inside and grabbed the wheel! The open black mouth of the garage loomed closer, only a few feet away. I didn't have time to think. I tried to find the brake but couldn't. David's hands left the bumper as the car got away from him.

"DARREN, STEER!" David cried out.

Somehow I hit the garage door opener. The garage door started coming down! I could see it closing and hear the grating metal spring. If that didn't wake Mom and Dad, nothing would.

The other car closed in, heading toward the driveway at ramming speed.

I felt my stomach go high into my throat as the wheels of our car bounced over the sill of the garage and inside. I saw a flash of wall and a dim light above.

I cut the wheel hard right.

I heard the sickening scrape of metal and felt my heart sink.

The car had stopped halfway in and half way out! I had to stop the garage door, but couldn't find the opener!

David hit the car from behind as hard as he could. It jerked and bounced, then slid the rest of the way in.

The horrid sound of scraping metal filled the garage. I saw sparks fly from between our car door and the garage door brackets. It sounded like the car door was coming off.

The light in the garage blew, plunging us into total darkness.

I yelped as the garage door closed.

Had David made it inside? Where was the other car? Was I okay?

I sat there for a moment as the darkness swam in inky circles before my eyes. Too quiet. My heart pounded. The car light came on, blinding me as the car door flew open.

Two hands grabbed me!

"Great job, Darren." David sneered, pulling me out of the car.

"What do you mean? You shoved the car in! Where have you been? Who's in that other car? What did you do? Are you wanted? Are you crazy?" My mind raced. I was still shaking from the last horrible moments.

David crept over to the garage door and carefully peeped out. I could barely see him in the dim light coming through the small twin windows in the garage door.

"They're gone," David muttered, sounding relieved.

"Who's gone? What's going on, you moron?" I demanded. My arms flapped up and down in sheer frustration.

David darted to the left side of the car

and ducked out of sight. I heard a startled gasp and something that sounded like a sob.

"David?" No reply. I walked slowly over to the side of the car and peeked around.

"Oh, no. Oh, no." David knelt beside the car, his finger tracing an enormous gash in the passenger door, about a foot long and three miles deep. Even in the dim light, I could see the jagged, raw edges. If a car could bleed, this one would have needed a hundred and eighty stitches. It might as well have had a blow torch taken to it.

I felt my jaw quivering uncontrollably. Tears welled up in my eyes. A gurgle escaped my throat.

"Oh, no." David, jumping to his feet, smacked his head with his palm. "We are so dead," he croaked.

"Where do you get that "we" stuff, partner?" I stammered. My life. Over in the eighth grade. I wouldn't see daylight until I was thirty. The rack. The iron maiden. The plank. The guillotine. Mere child's play compared to what surely awaited us.

"It must have scraped the side of the garage door on the way in. What are we going

28

to do? We can't hide this. Dad is going to see this and hemmorage." David grew panicky now. I, as usual, hatched a perfect plan. So logical. So brilliant.

"Let's run away," I said, envisioning a lifetime on the road. Week old hotdogs, rock soup and friends named "Bubba" or "Redeye".

"Oh, no. Oh, no." David buried his face in his hands, sounds of extreme pain and anguish dripped through his fingers.

It went beyond what happened to the car. I had seen David upset before but never this upset. He seemed really scared, and not just of being grounded for life.

"Who's after you, David?" I asked again, as steadily as I could.

David fixed me with a look of shock and horror, his face extremely pale and drawn. Cold sweat dotted his forehead.

His hand slowly raised and he pointed behind me. He mouthed one word that chilled me to the bone.

"Them."

It couldn't be. I ran to the window of the garage door as my jaw dropped open, my brother David right behind me, neither of us saying a word.

The same car that vanished at the video store and McDonald's was parked right in front of our house.

The strange old car shook like an angry old man. A faint blue glow surrounded it and a strange whirling mist blew through it.

Faded sea-green paint and huge rust spots held it together. The headlights flickered and blinked erratically.

It looked as if someone had sawed the roof off and replaced it with a floppy, ragged cloth top.

The sound coming from beneath its

dented hood was more of a grumble than an engine purr. It sounded like a bunch of tin cans being slung together.

I didn't see a driver.

But there were passengers.

Three ghastly teenagers sat in the back, almost on top of each other. I could see their faces clearly. All three stared intently at the house. More precisely, they stared into the garage, straight at us. No denying it. They grinned skull-like grins over rotted teeth.

"They can't see us. No way can they see us in here," David whispered.

All three of the ghostly passengers nodded slowly, as if in response.

We ran like crazy into the living room, tripping over each other, to the front window to get a better view.

Those three ghastly kids stared at us in the living room now.

"What did you do to make them mad, David?" I demanded.

"Nothing. I didn't do anything!" David said, reaching for the rod that closes the blinds. "They started following me. That's why I was gone so long. I kept driving around, trying to lose them."

"You didn't," I said, never taking my eyes off the car.

"No kidding," David said as he started to close the blinds. The car roared in response.

The three teenagers ducked down into the back.

"It's moving," I said in disbelief as I watched the flickering headlights turn slowly toward the house. The wheel turned without a driver! It made a wide U turn in the middle of street, circling back around like a shark.

"How is this happening?" I asked my genius brother as he yanked the blinds open with a snap, giving us a wide view of the car that had just left the street and was now tearing across our lawn toward the house.

The headlights caught us like deer. We couldn't move.

The car roared straight at the front window, refusing to stop.

"IT'S GOING TO RAM US!" David cried. He scrambled over the couch and toward the television, his eyes as large as the headlights that transfixed me.

My brain completely froze up as I stared at the front grill of a car speeding toward our living room window.

I could almost hear the glass shattering. A vast wall of glass, our living room window, would shower down on me, cutting me into a million shreds. I could practically feel my ribs crack as the front grill would hit me and send me flying into the wall.

The headlights bounced two inches from the window now. The clattering of the engine rang in my ears.

My brother grabbed me out of the way.

Then the unexplainable happened.

With a loud whoosh the car *passed* through the front window and wall and lurched to an abrupt halt in the middle of our living room. No shattering of glass. No crashing wall. No incredibly loud explosion. Not even a torn curtain. The lamp wobbled a little.

The car passed through the wall like it wasn't even there. Its engine idled so low, we could barely hear it. The headlights flickered and made two perfect circles of light on our bookcases.

A strange odor filled the room and the glowing blue mist that came from the car swirled around our ankles.

My brother, with his amazing knack for words, said the most appropriate thing for the moment.

"Whoa."

"You took the words right out of my mouth," I said.

We stood next to the passenger side window. We saw no one in the car.

Then a hideous head thrust out of the rear window and started laughing at us. The head of a disgusting teenage boy. His face stretched tight against his skull; his eyes huge and bulgy; his hair a black, stringy mess, matted and knotted.

David and I both yelped and fell back as two other teenage boys rose from the car; one a beefy blond with cruel eyes and a flat top so short, I saw his scalp pulsating. The other, a wiry redhead covered with so many freckles it took a moment to *find* his eyes. When I did, I wished I hadn't.

"David. Why'd you run off so fast, buddy?" the redhead cackled. His strange voice echoed like two people talking at once.

"Not very nice, David," the beefy blond said sorrowfully.

"We're going to kill you both," the skull-headed kid chirped.

"Shhhhhhh." The beefy blond held his finger to his bloated lips.

That last part got my full attention and woke me from my stupor. I felt a surge of panic. I was about to die. I grabbed David by the collar and yanked him close.

"David. These guys talk like they know you." He stared blankly and shook. "Do you know them?"

"I..."

The three ghostly boys slowly crept from the car, through the mist and toward us.

"I kind of hit their car," David continued. Three hideous heads bobbed up and down in gleeful confirmation.

"You what?" I asked as calmly as a person could, faced with death at the hands of three vile teenagers in a ghost car.

"I didn't see them. They popped up out of nowhere at McDonalds' parking lot. I came around the side of the building and WHAM! Only not wham," David said backing away from the advancing hoodlums.

"What do you mean, "not wham?"" I asked on the verge of tears. The one with the red hair curled his pointer finger at me. The fat one cracked his knuckles.

"I hit their car but I didn't *hit* their car," David said as he backed into the living room bookcase. Several volumes of Encyclopedia Britannica slid off the shelf behind him. "The car passed through their car...like it wasn't even there."

"But it was there, David. And now there's a new dent," the red haired kid growled. "You don't know our father, David. He won't believe it wasn't our fault. Not coming from us, anyway." The three lurched toward us, closing in for the kill.

The end. Game over. Vengeance city. I couldn't believe it. My idiot brother smashed into some ghost car and now its grisly occupants planned on murdering us in cold blood.

I couldn't believe my parents, still asleep upstairs! Did these hideous creeps do something to them? Why hadn't Dad woken up and come to our rescue? Then again, after he saw our car he'd have probably *helped* them take revenge on us.

Oh, we were so dead. Then, suddenly and without warning, David grew a backbone.

"Your car wasn't the only one damaged in the accident. Our father's not exactly a push over either," David snarled. "You ran out in front of me! Remember?"

The red haired kid suddenly stopped and held back the other two as well. It looked as if the most evil of thoughts had just crossed his warped mind. The mist curled about the room. The car in our living room sputtered a moment, then stopped.

"Hold it a minute. I have an idea," croaked the red headed kid.

A chill whipped through the room.

The red headed kid's eyes narrowed to two tiny slits that looked cut into his face.

"Let's look at your car," he said.

# 10

I felt the icy grip of the skull faced kid's hands around my shoulders, holding me in place. The fat kid held David. Their hands looked all shriveled, as if they had been under water for a long time.

The red haired kid traced the scratch on the side of the car with his long bony finger. He stood and smiled at us. His teeth, the few left unrotted, were as green as grass. I could have thrown up.

"Ever hear of Crest?" David kicked. No use. Their iron grips couldn't be broken.

The red haired kid went over the car from top to bottom, from side to side and inside out. At last he returned to his comrades. "Well, what do you guys think? Jaccob?"

"I like it, Silus. It gets good mileage and

has the trim aerodynamics of today's well-made Japanese import," Jaccob said thoughtfully.

"How about you, Squeeb?" he asked the skull faced kid.

"Though it's a family car, it still retains the tight control and road hugging action of its sport model counterparts," Squeeb said, tightening his grip. His breath smelled like rotted fish.

"The luxury of a family car with the precision of the leading sports model. I like it, too. Congratulations, Dave. You are one heck of a salesman."

Silus smacked his hands together and bounced over to David, inches from his face.

David looked beyond scared. We both felt absolutely powerless. Three creepy idiots talking about taking *our* car out of *our* garage and nothing we could do.

"We'll need all the paperwork. You know, the insurance, the registration, the title...all that stuff...oh, and all the spare keys," Silus said with a grin, his red hair waving hideously. "And I need you to sign a simple agreement."

"You can't be serious. We can't give you our car. Dad will kill us," David said.

"If you don't, *we'll* kill you," Squeeb cracked. Jaccob shushed him again.

"Fair's fair, Dave. You wreck our car, we take yours." Silus passed through the passenger side door with a weird whoosh and a swirl of mist. He drifted into the back seat and made himself comfortable.

"Lots of leg room," he said.

With a soft metallic clink, I set Mom's keys down on the living room coffee table. It joined all the paperwork the slime-bag asked for, as well as a set of keys that David snuck out of Dad's coat pocket, and the spare key that David used earlier.

"That's everything," he announced in total defeat. Squeeb, Jaccob and Silus smiled at the pile of stuff on the coffee table.

Silus produced a ratty piece of paper from his pocket, pale green and horribly stained. He handed it to David.

"Just sign on the dotted line and we're out of here," Silus said.

"I can't even read this." David held the

paper up to me. The words had smeared into a blurry blob. I couldn't read it either.

"What is it?" I asked.

"It's a simple agreement, signing your car over to us. That's all. Sign it!" Silus growled, nodding at Jaccob and Squeeb.

Jaccob grabbed David by the throat as Squeeb shoved a pen in his hand, forcing a scrawl from David's hand onto the paper.

"That's not fair. I didn't really sign that!" David protested.

"I guess that about does it. We'll leave our old car here with you. It wouldn't be fair otherwise, would it, Dave? After all, a trade's a trade," Silus said with an evil grin. He grabbed the stuff on the coffee table.

Their nasty old car sat silently between our couch and the fireplace. The glowing blue mist rose knee high in the room.

I darted a glance at the top of the stairs. No light. No Dad. No hope. These guys must have done something to make sure Mom and Dad wouldn't wake up. Or maybe I was asleep and dreaming this whole thing.

The light snapped on at the top of the stairs. Oh man! DAD WOKE UP! YES!

"DAVID! IT'S DAD!" I shouted.

The nasty old car in the middle of our living room changed right in front of our eyes.

The tall fins on its rear bumpers shrank. The grill narrowed. The bumper curled up into a smile. The mist enveloped it and blew back out and *there sat our Toyota Celica in its place.* The doors flew open wide.

*Their* car morphed into *our* car!

Silus jingled the keys, and they flew from his hand into the ignition switch. The headlights sprang on. The engine roared to life.

"DARREN DONALDSON! DAVID DONALDSON! What on earth is going on down there?!" Dad started down the stairs.

SAVED!

Or were we?

Silus, Jaccob and Squeeb piled in the back seat of the ghostly car that had morphed into our own. They peered out at us, smiling.

"Oh, one more thing..." Silus shouted.

The mist grew waist high in the living room now. We could barely hear Silus over the roar of the engine.

"Like I said before, about the accident?

Our old man would never believe it wasn't our fault. Not coming from us. But he might coming from *you!*" Silus screeched.

The mist rose high around us forming huge hands.

The hands, formed from the mist, shoved David and I into the car.

The doors slammed shut.

"Let's take a ride!" Silus screamed.

# 11

The car doors locked. My eyes shot forward as the car spun around in the middle of our living room, tires tearing our carpet.

The car stopped turning and the tires spun in place, held back by smoking brakes.

The front living room window loomed in front of us.

I could hear Dad's cry of fear and confusion from behind us as the car surged toward the wall.

"AHHHHH! We're gonna die!" David cried out as the front bumper hit the window.

I heard a weird whooshing sound in my head and everything went light. It felt like I didn't weigh anything. I couldn't feel my hands or my head.

I watched in amazement as the car

passed through the wall with me inside it!

A weird tingling coursed through my body as I found myself going through the wall with the rest of the car. I couldn't help it. I closed my eyes and screamed, even though it really didn't hurt. It felt like being underwater in a swimming pool. The feeling was so strange I barely noticed poor Dad pass out in the middle of the living room behind us.

We hit the street, taking the corner on two wheels! Street lights whizzed by so fast I could hardly see them.

I sat in the front next to the empty driver's seat, the steering wheel turning on its own. David sat right behind me, in some kind of shock.

"David, did you feel that? We went right through a wall. Are we dead?" I asked, the terror in my head growing. In the rear view, I saw the three goons' heads shake back and forth.

Not dead. Thank goodness.

All three goons pointed forward, out the front window.

AH! We'd just run a red light, straight for a minivan!

I looked over at the wheel and for a

moment, thought of grabbing it and turning but it'd already turned itself.

The three goons squealed with delight as we sailed past the minivan, furiously honking as it slid from the road and into a parked car. SMASH! The rear end of the minivan bounced straight up, it hit so hard.

"Some ride, huh kid?" Silus sneered.

"Where are you taking us, you stinking, ugly sack of slime? You have officially kidnapped us and our Dad *will* press charges," I cried out.

"We told you already, Junior," Jaccob said. "Our old man would kill us for wrecking the car. He'd never believe it wasn't our fault. You guys have to tell him for us. He'll believe you."

"And he'll love this new car," Squeeb cracked, rolling up the window.

"Sit back and enjoy the ride, kids. We'll be there soon enough."

My stomach lurched. The car smelled like rotted fish and sea water. As a matter of fact, the seats started to feel damp. Almost wet. The air in the car grew thick and smoky. It got hot, too. A weird blue glow covered everything. Green moss started to grow on the dashboard and the roof. I wondered if David noticed any of this.

I turned to ask, but the green cast to his face gave me my answer. Somehow he managed to speak.

"Don't worry, Darren. Dad'll report the car stolen and the police will pull us over any minute." David said. It sounded like he was trying to convince himself more than me.

Then an incredible thing started to happen. The car began changing again, only this time in reverse. The dashboard started to change from the nice sleek new dashboard to an old rotted cracked one. Then the instrument panel turned from hi-tech black and plastic to an old rusted steel with cracked glass.

*The car was morphing!*

Fins grew from the back bumpers and the color changed to a sickly sea green.

Then the top flew off.

I couldn't believe it. The wind whipped my face so hard, I almost cried. I heard the roof of our car bounce on the pavement.

As the rust grew and the engine

knocked, I realized that the car morphed from our nice, new Celica *back* to their rusted, old junker.

No way the police would know us now.

They had us again.

"That's better. Don't you think, boys?" Silus asked. The other two nodded.

"Does this mean our car's back in the garage?" David asked hopefully.

"Sorry, sport. A swap's a swap. This *is* your car. We just remodeled it a little," Silus laughed. "No, your Dad should be finding our old car in his garage right about now."

"This looks just like your hunk of junk now, creep! Why'd you even SWAP!" I yelled.

"No offense, Darren, but we have a certain style, and middle-class suburban doesn't cut it. Know what I mean? Isn't this better, anyway?"

I could see Dad in my mind, opening the garage door; frantically worried; ready to go looking for us, his two idiot sons, at three o'clock in the morning. There in the garage, he would find the ugliest piece of junk car ever unearthed. He would drop to his knees and cry to the heavens for his Celica and wonder what his two ex-children had done with it.

If only he could see it now, I thought to myself as the hood dented itself and a sickly green fender fell off.

"Don't look so depressed, guys. I KNOW WHAT!" Silus screamed. "Let's take one more spin through McDonald's parking lot, then we'll head to the boat.

Boat? What boat?

I read a book on pirates before I started my prize pirate ship model, as I said before.

The book scared me.

In it, a young boy is kidnapped by pirates and forced to serve as a cabin boy, basically a slave, while the pirates looked for secret treasure on an island in the South Pacific.

The boy had been *shanghaied*.

Shanghaied is when you are kidnapped to serve on a ship, usually a pirate ship. It didn't happen only to kids, either. Both men and women fell victim to this horrible experience. Starved and beaten, locked in cells below decks, they fought off rats, disease and each other.

If anyone died, they left them in the cell

with the survivors. Eventually, the survivors would lose their will to fight and would give in and become members of the crew.

I read in another book, a history book, that pirates would raid coastal villages for supplies. Slaves were looked upon as a supply just like water, food or gold. They could be sold or traded or kept to serve.

When the ship would drop anchor a mile or two from the coast, whole bands of pirates would board long boats and slip into the towns in the dead of night.

They would dock quietly and slink about the village, peering in windows and skulking along alleyways, looking for the unwary villager to bash over the head and take back to the ship in chains.

It didn't matter to them if anyone was dumb enough to be on the street in the dead of night. (Like a particular dumb brother I know.)

The pirates would slip into people's houses and steal their sons or daughters from their own beds (even if they were reading.)

If the rest of the family woke up and tried to stop them, the pirates would fight them off with swords and flint-lock guns and burn the house down using torches and lanterns.

On the way back to the anchored ship, some victims would get desperate and dive over the side into the water.

The crew would cheer and whistle as the poor victim desperately tried to swim away from the long boat and back to freedom. Their burning hometown would be in sight, but it wouldn't really matter.

No one ever made it back.

The pirates would cheer as eventually the victim would tire out and go under the waves for the final time or, if they were extremely unlucky, would go under in the company of a shark's fin.

*Shanghaied.*

Not me.

I would rather go over the side.

I grabbed for the car door handle.

I slammed into the cold hard pavement, rolling head over heels a couple of times as the car went on.

"DARREN!" I heard David cry as I felt the stinging and scraping on my hands and arms. No broken bones.

The car had been taking a turn around the side of the McDonald's, going just slow enough to mess me up real good. I was alive, bloody but alive.

As I stood up, I saw the car do a tremendous squealing, smoking U turn in the parking lot. It took a moment for me to get my senses back, but I couldn't mistake the horrible cackle of Squeeb in the back seat.

The car, furious over losing a prisoner, lit up a brilliant blue. Mist poured from its grill like smoke from a furnace. Its engine roared as it surged toward me. I had a split second to come up with a brilliant escape. One that Houdini himself would be proud of.

I ran. What else?

I rounded the building and hid against the huge order sign of the drive-thru. My back lit up red and yellow by the light behind me as moths and bugs swarmed all around, slamming their heads into every listed value meal on the menu.

I listened for the roar of an engine, but to my astonishment, heard nothing.

Where was the car? Waiting somewhere?

My heart throbbed as my pulse raced with fear. I wouldn't budge from the sign, the only light around. I couldn't hear the car. It had to be looking for me. They wouldn't give up.

I strained to listen but could hear only the sound of the bugs bumping and whacking the sign. Then suddenly the ordering speaker crackled to life beside me.

"WHAT IS GOING ON OUT THERE!" a voice boomed through the garbled speaker.

I screamed.

The car roared through the drive-thru, out of nowhere!

I saw a hand spring from the back window and grab my shirt collar. I sucked in a deep breath and pressed my back flat against the sign, trying to fight.

"One intensely unhappy meal to go," Squeeb cried as he yanked me into the car through the window.

We passed straight through the drive-thru as the manager dropped his broom and stuck his head through the little folding windows of window number two.

"YOU CRAZY KIDS! I'M CALLING THE LAW!"

The road. The town. All of it seemed to vanish as Squeeb thrust his ugly, deformed head in my face and yelled, "How did you do that?"

"Do what?" I yelped as he shoved me over the seat into the front.

David struggled against Jaccob who held him in his lap.

"How did you open that door?" Squeeb snarled.

"I don't know. I just did it!" I cried.

"They must still have something that belongs to this car," Jaccob snarled, keeping his arm solidly around David's throat.

"All right kid, what *haven't* you given us? We have to have everything! You understand? Everything!" Silus sounded furious. The car began sputtering and dying. Like it was running out of gas or having engine failure.

"Don't tell them, Darren," David choked, his throat pinched nearly closed.

"WHAT HAVEN'T YOU GIVEN US?" Silus' eyes glowed as blue as the car. He suddenly took on a weird, translucent look. I could see right through him! His clothes changed too. They changed from ratty old jeans and a T-shirt to a strange suit with a large collar. Almost like...an old time sailor's suit.

"Don't tell him!" David cried again.

I kept my mouth shut.

We swerved all over the road, the car out of control. We did a full 360° spin and through the windshield, I saw a concrete divider rapidly approaching.

Squeeb, his face awash with fear, tugged

at Silus' shirt. He desperately tried to get Silus to look out the windshield.

He wouldn't. He kept his eyes locked straight on me. He wouldn't flinch.

"What have you not given us, boy?" His voice took on a strange tone, like a voice from long ago that gained in strength. Silus didn't seem like a punk kid anymore. He became something more, inexplicably evil and ancient.

My lips curled over my teeth and I steadied myself for the impact of the wall.

"We gave you everything," I snapped.

Everything except another spare key Dad kept at his office.

The wall raced closer. In a moment, we would smash right into it.

Squeeb went nuts with fright, pulling at Silus' shirt. The tires squealed. Silus wouldn't look away from me. The headlights painted two perfect circles of light on the wall of closing concrete. The engine roared.

Squeeb screamed.

I smiled widely.

Remodeled or not, we had air bags.

"An extra key. It's at Dad's office," David cried at the last second.

The car instantly lurched back onto the road and the wall vanished from sight.

I was furious. "Why'd you tell him that, David?!" I couldn't believe it.

"I didn't want to be splattered on a wall like a bug," David said.

He could've been right. The Celica had airbags, but this wasn't exactly the Celica. Not anymore.

David reluctantly told them where Dad works. Before we knew it, we found ourselves zooming down the tree-lined driveway of Dad's office building complex. It's located at the edge of town with a small park, mini-mall and restaurants.

Little white lights hung from the trees and lined the roads leading to the parking garage. I had only been here about six times in my whole life.

The car lurched to a halt at a split in the road between the drop-off place out front and the parking garage. The car seemed to sag, sputtering like an old lawnmower.

Squeeb gently rubbed the seat cushion. "Better hurry, Silus." He sounded concerned.

A striped bar blocked the parking garage entrance. A vacant booth guarded the cavernous garage.

My anger grew. I didn't believe for a minute that we were only going with these guys to explain an accident to their father. An obvious lie! I knew they would never let us go. But why? They had our *car*. Why did they want *us*? I sure couldn't count on David. He wasn't fighting back at all. He got us in the mess in the first place because of his stupid pouting and his sneaking out.

Then Silus startled me.

"Which floor?" he asked gruffly.

I stuck my tongue out defiantly and he grabbed my face, squeezing it until my tongue came out further than normal. It hurt.

"Thirteenth floor," I gagged.

The car veered left and started straight toward the building. Fast.

"What are you doing?" I cried.

"Oh, no, Silus," Jaccob moaned.

"Oh yeah. Oh YEAH! YES!" Squeeb cried out excitedly.

The car bounced over the pavement toward the front of the building.

We went through a row of hedges. I mean we went *through* a row of hedges. No vanishing. No ghosting. We *tore* through the hedges in a very realistic sense, giving everyone in the car quite a bump.

"Oh, no. OH, NO!" David hid his eyes as we approached the front of the building.

We didn't slow down. This time the car remained very solid and very real.

"Don't, Silus. It's too d-d-dangerous," Jaccob stammered.

Silus didn't say a word. He seemed deep in concentration. The car glowed brilliantly and the mist poured around us.

"We're gonna HIT!" Squeeb screached.

The car hit the front stairs and we all tipped back into our seats as the front of the car went straight up. I felt a sick sensation in my stomach and an unsettling sense of speed as we rose.

Gravity pressed us flat into our seats. The engine raced and Squeeb squealed at the top of his lungs.

"D-D-David?" I stammered.

We were going straight up the wall.

We were driving straight up the wall of the building. I looked out the window and saw the tops of the street lights race away.

I felt an enormous pressure on me, like when you go up fast in an elevator. The wind slammed into the car and rocked it as it continued to climb. The engine strained. I couldn't be sure but I think everyone in the car became more terrified with each passing floor.

We drove up faster! I forced my head away from the seat and looked out the window, toward the building. The lights of the windows raced by, one after another. Office copiers and desks, potted plants and computer stations whisked by in a blur as we drove up the side of the building.

My ears filled with rushing air and popped loudly, my stomach pressed flat against my back. The wind buffeted the car as it climbed. My stomach heaved. My limbs locked in numbing horror.

Then we stopped.

We parked vertically on the side of the building thirteen stories up. I stared out the windshield at the starry sky, the back of my head planted firmly into the headrest.

No one said a word. No one moved a muscle. The car creaked and groaned, ready to roll back at any moment.

"Go get the keys," Silus said.

Remember my pirate book? Well, they did something else to people in the days of pirates. Something terrible. They called it walking the plank.

"Go get the keys," Silus croaked again.

The car creaked and groaned and complained, threatening to roll back any second.

"Are you talking to me?" A legitimate question.

"Go get the keys," he said again.

"You got legs. Go for it," I said with a false sense of bravado. I felt terrified.

The door beside me flung open and stopped with a creak. It stuck straight out to the side of the car, just waiting for an idiot to go walking on top of it.

"No way. David, this is your fault. You

go." I should've felt bad for saying it.

Without a word, David crawled over to the door and started to crawl up onto it.

"Hey, bro. I was only k-kidding," I stammered as David tested the car door with his weight. It gave a little, but looked like it would hold. The wind blew David's hair around like a crazy web.

"Don't do it, David! You're crazy! Get back in here!" I yelled.

"Shut up, Darren."

"Spare the heroics! You'll get yourself killed!" I cried. My brother, from the grump king to the prince of delusionary grandeur.

"How do you expect me to get inside?" David yelled as he carefully crawled on all fours to the middle of the door.

Squeeb moved past me and hit the car horn with his fist. . . hard.

*Every single window on the thirteenth floor blew out, raining glass in giant sheets.*

The car slid but David held his grip.

"Uh. Okay." David stood up carefully on the door. It was bending and creaking loudly.

It must have been a good two foot jump from the car door to the window frame, but when you're looking down thirteen stories, two feet might as well be two miles.

I held my breath as David tensed and everyone in the car leaned over, straining to watch.

The car lurched wildly to the side.

David lost his balance and flailed his arms in wide circles as he took the tiny little jump over that massive void.

He landed squarely inside the window. I can honestly say that at that moment, I had never been prouder of my brother's courage, and absolute stupidity.

David vanished into the darkness of the office. The office alarms sounded and I knew the police would be here soon.

If only we could find a way to hang on here for just a few moments, then we might have a chance.

If David could just find a hiding spot inside. Make them find him. Buy us some time. YEAH! He could "have trouble" finding the keys. Anything to stall until the police arrived.

David could do it. He could have been half way down to the lobby by now.

He would be a hero.

"If your brother doesn't bring us those keys very soon, we'll *all* be on the ground floor," Silus barked. "We have to have *everything* or we'll lose power over the car. It will be a regular car again, understand?"

The headlights flickered and the engine stalled, sending us sliding down in a terrifying free fall for a moment. WE ALL SCREAMED!

The lights kicked back on and the engine roared. We stopped.

"HURRY UP, DAVID! You weasel," I called. He'd better get back here and forget that hero stuff!

At last he came running out of the dark. He held the keys in his hand. Yes! I knew he wouldn't let me down.

He ran toward the shattered window.

The car lost power.

A scream escaped my lips as we free fell straight back. Everyone cried out! The wind. The falling sensation. My stomach smacked into my heart and both made it to my throat.

I felt myself floating from my seat as we fell, the seatbelt straining against my waist. Weightlessness. Helplessness.

David hit the edge of the window and jumped. He landed on the door with the help of the mist which seemed to pull him to it.

The door sprang shut and flipped David inside. Silus snatched the keys out of David's hand and the car engine roared to life.

The headlights snapped on. The brakes slammed into the floor, slowing our descent and we screeched down the last five stories, throwing sparks from under the car.

We hit the ground rear first, then rolled gently back. Our front end safely touched the ground with a bump and a bounce.

Everyone breathed a sigh of relief.

"We'd better get home. Dad's gonna start to wonder where we are," Jaccob said.

"You're right," Silus agreed, giving a nod to the steering wheel. "We'll be in trouble as it is. We're way over due."

"Yeah. We'll never get this duty again," Squeeb chirped.

Silus elbowed him to shut up.

"Where are you taking us?"

Silus, Jaccob and Squeeb looked over to me and smiled.

I shouldn't have asked.

# 16

Taverns; seedy dives on waterfronts; the favorite places for pirates to hang out and hunt people to shanghai to their ship. According to my book, entering the wrong tavern at the wrong time meant falling into the villainous hands of a pirate raiding party.

The wrong tavern.

Even McDonald's?

"Where are you taking us?" I asked again. The landscape blurred into a streak. With all the things belonging to the car in their hands, these guys could move at any speed. The needle on the speedometer had long since been buried off the scale. The steering wheel turned on its own. I felt sick again.

"We told you three times already. Home. Home. Home. We filled our quota. Don't you listen?" Jaccob said with his arms folded across his chest.

No longer allowed up front, I sat sandwiched between Jaccob and Squeeb. They both smelled like they had never heard of deodorant soap. Typical.

David sat quietly in the passenger seat, staring into space. Silus, also quiet, sat in the driver's seat, looking out the window. He didn't touch the steering wheel. From the back they kind of looked alike.

*A grimmer two there has never been...nor shall be again.*

Did that come out of *my* mind? I sounded like Silus. It could have been the ocean putting me in an old time sailor/poet mood.

*Wait a minute.*

*What ocean?*

The closest beach to Fairfield, Rocky Point Inlet, came into view in front of me. We made it in fifteen minutes. It should have been an eight hour drive without rest stops.

The lights of the Pavilion glowed in the distance. I could see the arcade and the roller coaster. Rocky Point all right. Impossible.

"David? This is...," I started.

"I know," David finished.

We zipped past the cheap strip hotels and the Holiday Inn where we stayed for a week in the summer. The ocean spread out in front of us. I saw the small white caps of the waves splashing on the dark sand. I smelled the salt air and saw the clouds drifting overhead. A mist covered the ocean.

A mist much like the one swirling about our car.

The bright lights of the main drag glared into the car. I loved coming here, under normal circumstances.

"You guys live on the strip. No wonder you cruise so well," I nervously remarked.

No response.

Dead silence.

"What's your Dad like anyway, Jaccob?" After all, we were going to meet the man.

Silus turned and answered for him. His eyes, glowing that weird blue again, turned practically transparent. His clothes changed and his hair blew about as if in a hurricane.

His voice cracked and thundered. His words seemed to be coming not from his mouth but from everywhere at once.

*"He is the ever livin' portrait of a doomed man. Ten heads tall, as thin and gaunt as a hickory candle. To look upon his face is to look upon a living skull, with eyes so pitch dark as to mirror the murkiest Nantucket night."*

The car took a sharp left, straight for the beach, the tires digging through the high piles of sand against the boardwalk wall. Despite our bouncing and spinning about, Silus never took his eyes off me and I didn't take my eyes away from him. He had me transfixed.

*"Forever lashed to the guide wheel that binds him. Forever staring at the dark and stormy sea that refuses him. Forever languishing in the visage of that night before him."*

I couldn't look away. Even as the car sped across the sand toward the lapping, growing waves of the ocean.

The doors locked.

*"Undaunted by the elements or the wrath of Neptune himself, around Cape Horn he did swear passage. Eight score and eleven men, pitiful wretches, did cry with anguish at their heartless captain. Their terrified pleas hung in the gale unanswered. This proud man,*

*said the doomed, who would by sheer pride
and stubbornness send us to a watery grave,
should suffer the fate of all ages and live in this
wretched storm forever more. Never seeking
port. Never the blessed footing of land shall he
know. This man who would round the Cape
against the will of nature and at the cost of his
crew and ship will forever challenge the Cape,
never to succeed."*

David cried out as the car hit the water.
The tall waves crashed across the windshield
and into the roofless car. The water passed
through Silus, who continued.

*"Cursed be he and his crew that perished
that night in the gale around Cape Horn. On
some nights such as this, far out to sea, a look-
out on a forecastle may cry to his shipmates,
Flying Dutchman ahoy! and that man may
shimmy down to join his crew standing aghast
at the railing, peering over the water and
through the murk to catch a glimpse of the red
light that hangs from her sails like fire.
Seething with the souls of the wretched, the
ship passes on its gloomy voyage. A sure sign of
disaster for any unfortunate crew unlucky
enough to sight the phantom ship and the*

*wicked man who helms her, lashed to the guide wheel forevermore,"* Silus concluded.

The car headed out to sea.

We pounded across the surf like a speed boat. The mist around the car formed a barrier of sorts and kept us afloat.

The front of the car rose in the air to crash down again and again against the waves.

David yelled as we plunged over and down a ten foot swell. I could barely see through the wall of spray and foam.

No land. No beachfront hotels. No rollercoaster. No arcade. Only high waves and rolling mist.

I held onto my seat as hard as I could. The window beside David and me cracked and broke against the pounding. The roar of the wind in our ears made it impossible to hear anything now. Drenched to the skin, I saw David open his mouth in something that could have been alarm . . . or awe.

I watched Silus raise his bony arm and point across the water.

I looked and almost fainted.

It stood in full relief against a dark red

glow, a black silhouette of gnarled masts and rigging. Sailors scurried across the rigging like spiders. It cast no reflection, and mist passed right through it. It made no noise, and gave me a chill that shook me to the bone.

*The Flying Dutchman.*

No doubt about it. There at the guide wheel stood a giant skeleton of a man.

Silus looked at it and then to me.

He mouthed one word.

"Dad."

# 17

Without a word, spectral hands as cold as the sea hauled us aboard the phantom boat. Ghostly crewmen lashed our car to the side of the great Flying Dutchman. I looked down one more time. The car had morphed again. This time into a ghostly blue long boat.

We boarded a total wreck. It looked like she had been out to sea for at least a hundred years. The black wood that made up the deck was nearly rotted through. Ropes and rigging hung about the masts like spider webs in a tangled mess no one could undo. I was afraid to move because it looked like the whole boat could collapse in on itself.

Jaccob led us toward the guide wheel on the top deck. As we walked I sensed that all eyes followed us.

The most ghastly crew you ever saw scrubbed the deck with some horrible dark liquid that smelled as rancid as stagnant water.

The crew's faces haunted me, white as snow with skin so wrinkled I could barely make out their features. Some had large, staring eyes that hung like golfballs in their soft, drooping flesh. I could not figure out how they moved the mops with their skeletal arms.

Jaccob stopped David with a slap to the chest. I looked up and saw the upper deck.

Silus whispered to someone with his head down, never once looking up. I didn't have to ask. I knew exactly who.

The Captain.

Everything Silus described him to be and more. I could barely make him out in silhouette and I'm glad of it. Only by the crack of lightning did I see any details of his face. A bit of bone here, a scrap of flesh there. Mostly I saw big bony teeth fixed in a permanent smile with no flesh to cover them. I never saw his eyes. Only a captain's hat on top of a long black overcoat, lashed to a steering wheel six feet across.

A quick shove from behind and we reluctantly climbed the ladders to the upper deck.

Silus stepped aside as we stood staring. Squeeb and Jaccob crawled up the ladders and slunk behind the captain.

I didn't know what to do. Terror prevented me from saying anything. I guess that's why my brother spoke first.

"Uh. Mr. Captain, sir. About your car..."

The figure raised his hand to silence David. Squeeb took the opportunity to speak.

"These are the guys, Daddy. These are the ones who wrecked the old car. They ruined our whole raid."

"Hey. You ran into me! Remember?" David growled.

"They'll make fine swabs after a time in the brig, Father. Particularly the fiesty, little one. Not a bad bit of shanghaiing, if I say so myself," Silus said.

Jaccob stammered, "How'd ,we do, Dad? Good? It's only two boys but they caused real trouble. I know it's not as many as we usually g-g-get but...."

The ghostly figure of the captain stopped them all with a raise of his hand and a turn of his head. I heard a sickening popping sound as he turned, like bones breaking.

Lightning flashed as the wheel turned beneath the ghostly captain's hands. The ship turned slowly amid the crashing waves

. . . and headed straight out to sea.

"HURRAY!" The three brothers cried.

If I didn't do something drastic and fast, our coastline would be a memory.

Like David and me.

I grabbed the wheel right through the captain and spun it with all my might.

"Way to go, Darren," David said as I stared between the rusted iron bars of the cell.

If my head had been shoved any tighter between the bars, I would never have gotten it back. I couldn't believe this. I remembered the tiny skeleton I glued on my pirate ship model. I remembered how cool I thought it looked and how much fun I had building it.

"Well we had to do something, didn't we?" I snapped back.

"You touched the man's wheel. It's no wonder we're in here, now," David said.

"Why didn't you stand up for yourself instead of letting Moe, Larry and Curly do all the talking?" I replied, as nastily as I could.

"You might as well have pulled his pants down and flipped his hat off," David groaned.

"They stopped me, remember?"

"Another two seconds and you'd have had us hanging by the yard arms, or whatever they call them!" David yelled.

"Another two seconds and you'll be eating a sea-faring fist," I yelled back.

"Oh yeah!" David yelled. He tackled me and we started going at it as usual.

We wrestled around for awhile until finally we both fell over from exhaustion. Neither of us had enough fight left in us to make it worthwhile.

We sat there for hours, it seemed. Not saying a word. We both just stared into space, listening to the creak of the boat and the splash of the ocean.

"I'm sorry, Darren," David said. I had to blink. I had to check my hearing. The first time that David ever apologized to me for anything. It got my attention.

"Really? You're sorry?"

"This is all my fault. Every stupid, last bit of it. If it wasn't for me we wouldn't be here. *The grump king* got us thrown in a brig. You aren't to blame for this. Not one little bit. It's about time the grump king is overthrown."

I think he actually meant it. He began to sound like the old David I knew.

"I dunno. I'm the one who spun the wheel of misfortune up there," I said smiling.

"Well, we had to do something, right?" David said with a grin. "You know, this looks a lot like that model you built."

"The one *you* didn't help on," I said.

"Yeah. Of all the ones for me to start acting like a jerk on, it had to be that one. I promise whatever *we* build *next*, will have secret exits galore in perfect detail."

The old David had definitely returned.

"Do you remember the layout of the one you built? Any way out? Secret panel? Anything?"

"No. Nothing." I started looking around the cell. Nothing at all. Some chained up skeletons against the wall. Some rats. Some rancid water they drank from. How could we escape?

I poked my head out of the bars and looked up and down the hallway.

Lots of cells, all lined up. They all seemed to be empty. Every single one but ours.

I slid back between the bars.

"Man. There is nothing out there. We're doomed. Doomed I tell you." I crouched down into a heap on the floor.

"There has to be a way out this. We just have to stick together. Come up with a plan. Think like a team."

David went through the pockets of the skeleton's clothes.

I raised a hopeful face to him as he shook his head.

Doomed.

Some team.

Then we heard the voice.

"Slop time. Come and get it," the voice squealed followed by a loud clatter on the floor.

I turned my head in time to catch some sloppy, gloppy white paste in the face. Yuck. It smelled like rotted fish, an odor I had become very familiar with that evening. The food bucket hit the floor in front of us and bounced to the side, losing its grisly contents.

"Ohhh, gross. What's this?"

"Who . . . ?," David asked as he pushed his way past me toward the small, withered shape peering at us through the bars.

Outside our cell, stood an old man with long white hair and amazingly wrinkled skin.

A patch covered one eye, and the other, milky white with no pupil, popped out a little too far from the socket. His bald head seemed pieced together by scars. He wore a ratty red striped shirt and short pants. He couldn't have been over four feet tall.

"Who are you?" David asked.

"Wouldn't you be meaning how do you get out of here?" The old man asked with a cackle. He kicked the bucket to the side and laughed at David outright.

"Yeah. That's what I meant. How do we get out of here?" David asked

The old man shook and smiled, his teeth rotted and green. Oh man, it would make you gag to look at them.

He pointed a long bony arm which popped out a shriveled little hand which extended a crumpled finger, pointing behind us.

We turned to look and saw only the skeletons lying chained to the floor, grinning up at us stupidly, as if they knew a dreadful secret.

"We ram the skeleton's head through the ship wall and swim back to land?" I gulped.

"NO! No. No!" The old man shouted angrily, stomping about.

"We use the skeleton's bony finger to pick the lock when you leave?" David said excitedly.

"NO! You idiots. You die. YOU DIE!" The old man stomped around furiously, fit to be tied. "Never in me born days have I seen two sorrier, soggy sacks of stupidity spat up by the sea. You two have been driven to DEATH! Don't you see that? A living death more wretched than the foulest fiend could imagine. Forever lost at sea."

The old man looked pleased with himself as he thrust his hideous face closer to the bars, laughing at our doom.

"WAIT! I have it," David exclaimed again. He grabbed the old man through the bars and pulled him hard into them, knocking him stone cold with a loud THWACK.

"First we knock the old man out!" David said, pulling the body closer.

"Okay. That you did. Good job," I said checking over his work. "What next?"

"Then we search him for the key and unlock the cell door. Then we make our way to the upper deck!" David gingerly searched the old man's pockets, pulling back the shirt like you would a newspaper off a dead fish.

I yelped as the old man's arm shot up and grabbed David's hand! His eye popped open and his lips shot back, revealing his green teeth.

"I don't have a key! Hee hee hee hee!" the old man cackled.

David yanked his arm back with disgust, holding it close, happy to have it back.

"You can't harm a ghost, boy." The old man leaped to his feet. "My real body is in the cell at the end of the hall, chained tight as a drum to the floor where it's been for a hundred years, though there ain't much left of it to keep."

"Ugh! That's disgusting!" David jerked away from the bars.

"Please, mister. Can't you help us? I need to get back home. We have parents who will worry. I was going to get my driver's license in a year and a half. Please. . . Help me," I begged.

David hit me in the chest.

"Us, I mean."

I gave the old man the most absolute, soul-stirring, heart-wrenching, ice-melting, warm-fuzzy-puppy-eyed look I could muster. It had to work. It hurt. My eyes teared up. My face muscles ached with regretful pleading.

"Weeeellllll . . ." The old man rubbed his chin, thoughtfully.

I had him. I HAD HIM!

"I can't!" He exploded with laughter.

I hung my head in shame. That trick had netted me countless comic books, basketball shoes and advances on allowances, but here in the clutch when everything mattered, I'd blown it. Air ball.

"Tell you what, though." The old man leaned toward the bars.

We leaned in closer as well.

"Are you betting boys? Do ye fancy a wager every now and again?" The old man asked with a wink.

"Maybe," David said cautiously.

Oh, no. David was notorious for losing bets. He once had to run through the middle of a football pep rally in a dress, because he made a bet on who could bench-press skinny Joe Alister the most times. Shelly Miller is a lot stronger than she looks.

"When the duty masters come a calling,

ye best pay heed and bow to the whip and whistle, lest you end up like the poor bilge rats behind ye. And when there be a game afoot. . . make your wager. They'll answer yer challenge, the captain's three wee brats, I mean." The old man winked his one eye and started down the hall, the lantern swaying with every unsteady step.

"Wait! What do we bet? What do we play?" David called, his face pinched between the bars.

We could barely make out what the old man said. *"A contest of courage is what they'll be looking for. Dare a game of chicken! You'll play by their own special rules, unfair and uneven. Bear in mind, you'll always turn the odds to your favor when you count on each other. The home-field advantage be yours."*

The old man laughed until he vanished completely.

## 20

It became routine after awhile. We would drift through the dark and eerie fog, only to mysteriously emerge, frightening some fishing boat or luxury liner or Navy patrol vessel.

Yeah. yeah. yeah. Nothing spooky about it to me or David. Our hands dripped bloody and raw from the wire scraping bristles of the brushes we clutched. How many planks could be on this stupid boat and how clean could we possibly get them? A short crack of a whip and my mind shot back to my duties.

The whip master with the bo's'n whistle around his neck scowled at us. His glowing red eyes narrowed as I looked right through his ghostly form at the rest of the poor wretches swabbing the lower decks. They'd been going for hours without a break.

"You missed a spot, Mr. Attention-to-Detail." David cracked, shoving his arm right past me.

"Shut up, all right," I sneered.

"GET BACK TO WORK!" the whipmaster growled as he cracked the whip in front of us again. He worked us harder than Coach Dawson ever did.

"Darren, check it out." David pointed at a growing crowd of sailors and pirates bustling around Silus, Squeeb and Jaccob. They seemed to be rolling something on the deck and it sure wasn't a mop.

"This must have been what the old man meant," David whispered, never taking his eyes off his scrubbing. "We have to get down there somehow."

My hand shot up and I looked at the whip master with wide, anxious eyes.

"Pee break!"

The next thing I knew David and I pushed and shoved our way through the meanest, mangiest ghost crew ever assembled.

Squeeb knelt at the head of the crowd.

Everyone watched Squeeb's cupped hands nervously as he shook them up and down, up and down, in preparation to toss whatever horror he had hidden. I sensed a strange electricity pulsing through the crowd with every bounce of his bony hands.

Suddenly a pair of dice, carved from bone, rolled and tumbled across the rotted flooring, finally revealing . . . a five and a two. A great groan swelled from the crowd as twenty men dropped like lifeless lumps onto the wooden deck.

"Drat my accursed luck," I heard one cry as he settled on the floor with a thud.

"Ha, HA!" Squeeb cried with glee as the dice came back to him. "Number seven again. Lady luck is spitting on my head tonight. Ptooooie!"

The scumbag spat right on the deck. I would wind up cleaning it later.

"Well. Look what we have here, boys. If it ain't the newest members of our jolly crew. What say ye lads? Have a go at the bones? A far better gamble than signing your name on a paper ye haven't even read. You didn't think twice then, so why now? . . .

. . . Or do ye have the guts?"

Silus stood and crossed his arms, staring at us. The crew gathered tight around him, but not too close. Nobody touched him. The captain's favorite, I heard someone say.

"I want our Dad's car back and I want to go home." David had never sounded braver. He stared at Silus with bulldog determination and mule stubbornness.

"OHHH! He names the stakes, says I. But what be the lay in turn?" Silus asked to the crowds amusement.

"What? I don't understand a stupid seafaring word you're saying," David snarled.

The crowd seemed to like that, though they clearly wouldn't dare laugh out loud.

"What will *you* bet, moron? And it better be good," Squeeb growled.

Squeeb wasn't kidding. This ship wanted blood. I could feel the tension in the air. The crew became still. What could we possibly bet? David's eyes narrowed. He cleared his throat and wiped the sweat on his forehead. His hair blew in tangles around his face as clouds churned overhead and lightning split the sky.

Our lives hinged on whatever David said next. Our wager had to be drastic enough to get their serious attention. How do you match the stakes of the damned, after all? He needed to *surpass* their grim situation, in the terms and expressions a pirate could understand. Tough call. I only hoped that he could pull it off.

I held my breath.

David began to speak.

"If we lose, we will remain aboard this ship forever. Slaves. Worse than slaves. Sapped of our will and forced to serve our master's bidding. The chains on our broken hearts will be as big as those on the anchor and will rattle in our souls and the souls of those we leave behind. Those unfortunate sailors who witness our passing on the bow of this phantom ship will be forever haunted by our grim staring figures. They will recall our faces each night in their restless sleep. Our eyes will stare at them through a cloudy haze, limp in their dark sockets. Sadness without equal. Regret without end. Anguish as deep as the ocean. They will remember our faces *forever*... and *never* without a shudder. That's what I bet, for my brother and me."

"Woooaahhhh," cried the crew.

"Thanks a lot, Dave. Good job," I said.

"Nah. No. No. You're going to do *that* anyway! What will you *bet*?" Squeeb asked again.

"Oh wait. I have an idea," Silus cried. "You will gut every fish we pull from the waters from now until the end of time!"

I read in a history book once that the fish gutters on board a pirate vessel had the worst job of all.

Imagine sitting on the top of the biggest, stinkiest, slimiest pile of fish you could climb. Now imagine the heat in that lower galley. No windows. Locked doors. No air. No light. Your only company is the overpowering stench of muggy, rotting fish as you grope around in the musty darkness.

Now imagine reaching into that pile below you and grabbing the biggest, floppiest, ugliest flounder you could find.

With the fish in one hand and the fillet knife in the other you split it open.

With your raw, shriveled hands, you pull the insides out, tossing them onto another stinking, steaming pink pile beside you.

"It's a bet," David said.

The crowd cheered.

## 21

We, as the challengers, could pick whatever game we wanted. I sensed a lot of discomfort and nervous tension on deck as David and I quietly conferred about what to play.

The crew busily placed side bets while the wonder triplets glared at us for taking so long to decide.

"Anytime, ladies," Jaccob catcalled.

"Let's go!" Squeeb cried.

An enormous rotten net rose behind them. . . loaded with fish. Hundreds and hundreds of fish. The ropes could barely support the weight, creaking and groaning under the strain. Silus looked from the net being hoisted overhead to us and smiled.

"Oh, man." David looked ready to lose it. "We gotta think of something fast. We're going to wind up working for the Long John Silver's of the living dead forever. "

We thought of plenty of challenges, but our opponents had a distinct advantage being dead and supernatural and all. Dodgeball was out, for sure. Another tough call.

"Wait. Remember what the old man said?" David lit up. "Chicken! He said to play chicken. That's what we have to play!"

"I stink at chicken fighting." I remembered chicken fighting at school on the mat in the gym. We did it sometimes in place of wrestling. Always me, the one on somebody's shoulders with the foam bat. I remembered quick whaps to the head and the hard sting of the mat. I saw the ceiling of that stupid gym more times than I saw the wall.

"I don't think he meant chicken fighting like we know it, Darren," David said. "It's gonna be their rules and whatever it is, they'll definitely cheat. We're a team. We'll win if we stick together."

David sucked in a tremendous gulp of musty sea air and bellowed at the top of his lungs across the ship for all to hear. "THE GAME IS CHICKEN!"

It practically shook the ragged sails.

David looked across the deck from where we stood, past the crew that stared blankly, stunned at his choice of challenges.

He looked past the three idiots who had brought us here in the first place. They stood up straight, as if in answer to an *extremely serious* challenge.

He looked past the battered hold and the web of tangled rigging; past the rusty cannons and the rotted timber of the masts; past the swaying nets of fish and the ghostly wretches who attended them.

David looked up to the gigantic captain's wheel and to the ghastly figure forever lashed to it.

That dark shadow of a man turned its skeletal head with what seemed to be a superhuman effort, the sea itself responding to the movement. The captain nodded.

The challenge had been approved ...

Silus and his friends nodded in turn to their captain.

...and accepted.

## 22

My eyes couldn't look away from her. After hundreds of years on an uneasy sea, the battered, decaying old ship still held a magic. I almost felt a twinge of regret for leaving.

Our ghostly shipmates lowered us down by ropes to the glowing blue form of the long boat, still banging against the ship's side.

My eyes drifted from the lanterns hanging on the railing, to the tall masts in strong relief against a reddening sky.

I took my seat first. David sat next, followed by Silus, Jaccob and Squeeb.

As the long boat drifted away from the ship, I looked back at the towering form of the man at the wheel.

I felt an overwhelming sorrow for him. Oblivious to all those men scurrying around him by his own harsh command. He couldn't hear them or see them or feel them. Not really. Not the way you or I do. He wanted his dream badly enough to sacrifice everything, even his own friends and family, to reach it.

And he didn't reach it.

He lost everything instead, including his life and soul. I wish I could have asked him if it was worth it.

The ship stood silhouetted in red against the mist for another moment and then it vanished. Swallowed up by the sea again, like a candle's flame snuffed by a breeze.

No one said anything for a long time.

The bow of our long boat hit the sandy shore, followed by four radial tires that went tearing across the sand toward the lights of the strip. The boat completed morphing into the crummy old car again, complete with fins and rag-top roof.

"Don't get any bright ideas. Remember *you* pick the place but *we* make the rules," Silus growled from the back.

"We know. We know. Just get us there quick all right? I want to go home," David said.

"Don't worry. The ship will always be there for you," Squeeb squealed, poking his head between the seats. He tried to rattle us. To make us even more scared and upset.

I punched him in the ear.

"OW! You little snot. You just wait. I hope you like fish...inside and out." Squeeb sulked back into his corner.

"Settle down, Darren," David whispered.

We settled back into our seats in the front. "We'll get our chance. As long as we stick together." We watched the street lights whiz by at amazing speeds, even faster than before.

"What are the rules?" David asked.

"It's simple, really. We come after you and you come after us. Chicken. If you're still alive when it's over, you win!" Jaccob said rolling his window down and spitting outside.

"How do we come after you? That's not fair at all! It's impossible!" I exclaimed.

"That's your problem, ain't it?" Squeeb snarled. "Besides, we weren't talking to *you* now, were we?"

I could tell David didn't like the sound of that. He hadn't even worn his running shoes.

Potter's field, near the interstate, stretched out like an endless sea of tall grass, flowing up one hill and down the other, beside a chain link fence and a stretch of highway.

The only interruption of its sea green surface, an occasional abandoned car or other forgotten relic dumped there by the uncaring citizens of Fairfield.

On some nights, in the middle of Potter's field, you could see the lights of our street across the overpass bridge about a mile and a half away.

I watched David look for them as he stood on a grassy hillside...

a hundred yards away.

I sat in the back of the car with Jaccob, struggling for a view between the seats. Silus and Squeeb leered at David from the front.

Squeeb got his attention with the blast of the car horn. The headlights sprang on and held him in place. He looked cold, too terrified for words.

"Are you about ready?" Squeeb yelled.

He nodded and dug his foot into the ground, as if the wind could blow him over.

I felt dread swell in my throat. They would run him down and he wouldn't have a chance. I had to do something. But what?

The car engine roared and the tires spun, held back by the straining of the brakes.

How did I get into this? From reading comics in bed to scrubbing the deck of a nasty old ship to mowing my own brother down in my father's car. Not a good night.

I became their extra car insurance, they said, so David wouldn't run off. He stared at me through the front windshield with terrified eyes. I must have looked pretty pitiful myself. Nothing he or I could do. We both knew it.

The car engine roared and David crouched a little lower, rocking on his feet like a runner.

I could imagine the car grill. curving back like an animal's lips unsheathing its fangs and the headlights dimming as if to squint, showing it meant business.

Silus, Squeeb, and Jaccob leaned foreward in anticipation. The car reared back and forth like a runner, waiting for the sound of the starting gun.

The air grew thick with anticipation.

The roar of the engine, the sound of my breathing and the sense of incredible danger. Two beings, one of metal and glass, one of flesh and bone. My brother versus the machine.

The hunter and the hunted.

Then suddenly, "GO!" escaped from Squeeb with shouted glee.

The car lunged forward!

David...

ran like crazy toward the chainlink fence, heading straight for home.

What else could he do?

I watched the grass disappear beneath his feet as he plowed across the field, captured in the headlights.

Angry shouts came from the front seat as unintentional gasps left my throat. My heart ran faster than David. Tears filled my eyes. Helpless anger knotted my stomach.

The car swerved through the grass, taking a sharp left to cut him off, flinging me wildly across the seat.

"RUN, BOY! RUN!" Silus cracked.

The car gained on David, inches from his back in a matter of moments. My pulse raced and my heart pounded.

He would never make it. He couldn't run fast enough. He would never reach that fence before the car caught him and sent him sailing into the air, every bone in his body shattered.

I glanced around desperately.

Old man Duprey's rotted junker poked up from the grass, the only thing within running distance. The old Volkswagon bug had been there for as long as I could remember.

David had no choice.

No way he would reach the fence.

"RUN FOR THE BUG! DAVID! RUN FOR THE BUG!" I shouted from the car. Jaccob knocked me away from the window.

David turned and headed for the rusted-out old relic.

The car just missed him as he turned. It would be hard for it to turn in the grass, which bought him an extra few seconds.

He ran up to the skeleton of the old buried Volkswagon, propped up on cinder blocks, and dived into the open window.

"GET HIM!" Silus yelled.

Bright beams from the headlights hit the side of the bug as the car straightened out, picking up speed.

"LEAVE HIM ALONE!" I yelled. Jaccob laughed and shoved me against the window.

I saw David's head poke up, looking out the rusted Volkswagon window.

"NO!" I screamed. The car gained speed. The lights intensified on the rusted door as David's head disappeared. "DAVID GET OUT OF THERE!"

My terrified eyes grew wide as a deafening roar filled my ears. They wouldn't stop!

I ducked down.

Squeeb let out a horrid, excited scream as the car sped up...

and SMASHED into the Volkswagon.

The rusted old relic disintegrated on impact into a big cloud of metal shards and glass splinters.

The ghost car plowed through the mess, bouncing and jerking wildly.

The larger chunks seemed to hang in the moonlight for a moment, before crashing to the ground. It sounded as if a bomb went off.

"WAHOO!" Squeeb cried. "WE WON!"

"YES!" Jaccob proclaimed.

I cried out in disbelief. They had won. *I'd never see David again.*

My fault. I didn't do anything to stop them. My stomach hollowed and lurched. I couldn't breathe. *They killed David.*

"Wait a minute," Silus cried while looking out the driver's side window. "Hold on! THERE HE IS!"

He pointed toward a patch of grass ten feet away where David had sprung up, running even faster toward the fence.

The floor of the Volkswagon must have rotted clean through! YES! I could see the cinder blocks it must have been sitting on! David had crawled out before we even hit! A wave of relief washed over me.

"ALL RIGHT DAVID! RUN! RUN!" I cried happily.

I watched as he clutched the fence and scrambled over. He would reach the overpass bridge and have a straight shot for home.

The overpass bridge spanned the highway, about twenty five feet down.

"TURN! TURN!" Silus yelled.

The steering wheel followed the order.

"Little Brat. We'll catch him on the bridge. Squeeb! Give me the gun! Let's cheat," Silus cried excitedly as the car swerved away from the fence, tearing up a grassy hill toward the bridge.

Squeeb popped the glove compartment and started fishing around. He threw everything everywhere. Silus and Jaccob strained their glowing red eyes to keep up with David. The nothing that drove the car yanked the wheel furiously.

I watched David head across the bridge. I could see the lights of my street far off in the distance.

A sudden burst of anxiousness jolted me. Even if David made it home, what then? Would these guys let him go? No way. We could be putting Mom and Dad in serious danger. I'm sure he thought of that, too. But what else could we do? We couldn't just give up. Home seemed like all we had.

The lights of the car lined up on David's back as we straightened out again.

"I can't find anything in here!" Squeeb complained as he threw bottles and socks and maps over his head into the backseat. I covered my head to keep from getting pounded by the pile of garbage that rained down.

With the glove compartment completely

emptied, Squeeb cried, "OH! HERE IT IS!" and proceeded to pull out an ancient musket, the type of guns that pirates used. The barrel kept coming out of the glove compartment, more and more and more as Squeeb pulled. The tip of the gun emerged. A full forty inches long!

The musket could only fire a single shot and it wasn't a bullet. More like a little metal ball, a ball bearing. It came out in a cloud of smoke with an enormous kick.

*I had to do something. I couldn't sit by and let David be shot! But what?*

Squeeb lined up on David, swinging the gun to aim through the windshield.

"NO! YOU IDIOT! Silus cried.

"I've got him!" Squeeb yelled as he squeezed the trigger. I quickly grabbed the latch beside Squeeb's seat and pulled it.

The windshield of the car exploded and the whole car filled with an acrid smoke. The kick from the gun knocked Squeeb's seat into a full recline. I just barely managed to dodge it.

It worked. He missed.

The car swerved toward the side of the bridge, the front end threatening to go through the wall and over the side.

Everyone in the car screamed. The nothing driving yanked the wheel hard and pulled it back onto the road where it just
. . . stopped.

Suddenly.

Just like that.

The car stopped at the bridge.

We watched through the shattered windshield as David neared the opposite end of the bridge. He had made it. A chance.

"You'll never catch him now," I cried.

The glowing mist that surrounded the car snaked out and blew across the bridge, forming two giant hands as it unfurled.

"What? What's going on?" I asked as the car trembled. I felt myself rise on the seat as the interior stretched and unfolded, the mist blowing through in thick clouds.

*The car started morphing again.*

I looked up and saw two giant hands grab David from behind; stopping him; lifting him in the air and turning him around.

The hands were made of *mist*. The same mist that sucked David into the car at my Dad's office. The same mist that stopped the water from flooding the car at sea. The mist arms stretched all the way back up the bridge, back up to... *our truck*.

The car morphed into a glowing blue truck. An eighteen ton truck.

A semi... and I sat in the cab!

It crackled with a strange energy. Small bursts of electricity ran down the chrome, across the panels and into the steering wheel.

Jaccob threw me into the back of the cab with the garbage as he climbed forward, joining Silus and Squeeb.

"This is more like it," he laughed. They all high-fived.

I shot up and stared out the windshield between them. The mist hands held David's feet to the ground. He couldn't move. Couldn't run. They made him a sitting duck.

"HOLD ON!" Silus screamed. Jaccob and Squeeb joined him.

This time they couldn't miss. David would end up as a hood ornament if I didn't come up with something fast! *I coudn't think.* Fear had frozen me. My hands trembled. My mind blanked. *David's life depended on me.*

Then I saw the pile of stuff we gave them at the house. The insurance papers. The spare keys. The title. The contract

*... the contract.*

I grabbed the contract, folding it quickly, as fast as I could.

The truck fired up and started roaring down the bridge. David struggled against the mist but couldn't move. The two mist fists held his legs firmly. I could almost see the terror in his face as the lights struck him. He jerked and pulled frantically at the fists but could not pull free.

I had one shot.

I folded the paper in my trembling hands. Silus, Jaccob and Squeeb, too busy watching out the front to see me, reveled in their victory.

"We got him now!" Squeeb cried.

"We can't lose!" Jaccob yelled.

The truck hurtled toward him

....faster...faster...faster. I could feel us leaving the ground. Surrounded by mist and a crackling electrical charge like lightning, we barely skimmed the pavement. It felt like being on an eighteen ton stone thrown across a pond.

*David had eight seconds to live.*

I threw it from the window. A piece of paper, folded into a plane and flying through the air. It shot out of the back window and passed through the mist that surrounded it. It lit up a brilliant blue as it glided toward David.

I could only hope he would catch it.

It spiraled through the air. Ahead of the truck by inches, each spiral growing larger.

Something helped the plane.

Something guided it.

*David would be under the truck in moments. Catch it, David.*

"THE CONTRACT!" I yelled.

David's hands snatched the paper plane right out of the air. A miracle.

As soon as the paper landed in his hand, a brilliant flash of light enveloped us and the truck instantly morphed into the old car!

The car sputtered, a terrified Silus,

Jaccob, and Squeeb cried out as it hurtled out of control.

They had lost control over the car. *They didn't have everything anymore!*

I sprang from the back and grabbed the wheel, turning it with a tremendous jerk as David jumped out of the way.

The car went straight over the side of the bridge with me in it.

I cried out as I plummeted, weightless, holding onto the wheel for dear life!

I closed my eyes and braced for impact. I felt papers and garbage blow into my face. The sound of screaming filled my ears.

The front end of the car *passed* slowly and softly into the pavement with a bright swirl of mist.

I squeezed out from the ghostly trunk as the last of the car vanished into the earth with only a misty swirl remaining.

My pulse raced as a weird tingle coursed through my body. Small wisps of mist clung to my hands and around my legs, before evaporating into the air.

Holding my breath, I struggled to my feet and ran to the side of the road.

*The car had disappeared into the ground completely. No sign of it anywhere.*

David waved down at me, the contract clinched in his hand.

We won.

## 24

David held the contract tightly in his hand as he ran down the bridge toward me, a broad smile on his face.

We exchanged excited stories about our great victory and hugged for the first time in a long time. Bruised, battered and scared as could be but *alive*! More than I could say for...

Then we heard the clunker.

We looked down the bridge and saw the old car, banged up, heading toward us, dragging a muffler on the ground and sending out a shower of sparks to all sides.

A very depressed Silus, Jaccob and Squeeb sat in the back seat, much like the first time we saw them.

The wheels wobbled and the bumper grated the ground. One headlight had blown out and the engine coughed and sputtered. In a word, shot. It had lost the glow, and the mist that once empowered it shrank to a wisp.

They stopped beside us.

David casually strolled over and leaned against the side, sticking his head in the window. A tense, nervous silence hung in the car. Neither Silus, Squeeb nor Jaccob looked at each other.

They seemed terribly embarrassed.

"You won," Silus said looking at the contract in David's hand.

"I know," David replied unable to contain the smile that spread across his face.

"Oh. Just give them their stuff back, Squeeb," Silus said stepping out of the car.

Squeeb handed David the insurance, the extra keys and everything else that belonged to the car.

"I'm sorry for any inconvenience we may have caused you, sir," Squeeb noted in a voice that was not his.

"Yes. Terribly sorry," Jaccob chimed in.

Silus grumbled and stared at the contract in David's hand.

"Go ahead. What are you waiting for," he

said, shifiting his eyes to the car.

David smiled and handed me the contract. "I don't feel like driving. Darren, care to do the honors?"

"My pleasure," I said ripping the contract down the middle.

The car let out a huge groan of metal and transformed back into a nice, shiny Celica. Even the scratch in the door *we* caused had disappeared. As good as new.

We were off the hook!

David and I got in, closing the car doors with a certain satisfaction.

Three very unhappy ghosts stood by the side of the road with their hands in their pockets, their heads hung low.

David leaned past me, asking "You guys need a drop-off somewhere?"

Silus replied, "Naw. We got a ride."

I noticed a black Cadillac pulling up beside us, the windows tinted black, a license plate with the letters "FLYDTCHM".

"David?"

He shrugged.

Silus, Jaccob and Squeeb marched over to the Cadillac and climbed inside, not saying a word.

Silus sat up front, sulking in his seat. Pouting like a grump king.

The power window rolled down with a pneumatic sigh and we saw the old man from the boat behind the wheel!

He still had one eye and that patch and the ugly striped shirt. He looked to the three sulking bullies in his car.

"Wave good-bye, boys," he said to his grumpy passengers. They didn't look up.

The old man pulled on a familiar captain's hat and smiled.

"Don't mind them. They hate to be seen in public with their old man, know what I mean? I'll wave for them." He waved and laughed as he drove off.

His laughter remained as we watched the car move down the bridge and vanish with a red glow.

"Oh, man, Darren look at that!" David exclaimed pointing at Potter's field. We both had to get out of the car to watch. We watched together, though it lasted only an instant.

*It's been said that on the night of November 7, 1995, a phantom ship, the Flying Dutchman herself, sailed the grassy seas of Potter's field.*

# About the Authors

**Marty M. Engle** and **Johnny Ray Barnes Jr.**, graduates of the Art Institute of Atlanta, are the creators, writers, designers and illustrators of the **Strange Matter®** series and the **Strange Matter® World Wide Web page.**

Their interests and expertise range from state of the art 3-D computer graphics and interactive multi-media, to books and scripts (television and motion picture).

Marty lives in La Jolla, California with his wife Jana and twin terror pets, Polly and Oreo.

Johnny Ray lives in Tierrasanta, California and spends every free moment with his fiancée, Meredith.

And now
an exciting preview
of the next

#4 A Place to Hide

by Johnny Ray Barnes Jr.

# 1

The whole thing seemed like a bad dream. Thinking back, twelve-year-old Trey Porter would never have guessed he could end up this way.

He settled into the tallest cedar he could find. The wind blew harder, making the tree sway frightfully. Trey thought about the fifteen minutes it had taken him to climb to his perch. Nothing, absolutely nothing, nature could throw at him was going to make him climb back down.

Not with those Things out there. Those Woodlizards.

Trey looked down. What if he fell asleep? At the very least he'd crash to the ground and break a couple of bones. That was nothing compared to what the Woodlizards would do to him, though. No, he wouldn't fall asleep. Trey doubted if he would ever sleep again.

He scanned the area around his tree, straining to hear even the quietest whisper. If a rat breathed, he would know it.

He was hungry, too. Really hungry. His stomach growled so loudly that Trey was sure the Woodlizards could hear it. He tried to keep his mind on other things. Like his parents.

But he might never see his mother again. Or his father. He considered this, too. Being trapped in one of the largest forests in the state, with Woodlizards after him, was definitely having a bad effect on Trey's outlook.

If he ever got out of this mess, Trey swore he would round up a posse and come hunt those Woodlizards down. He would find every rifle-toting hunter within area and bring them out here to put an end to these fiendish creatures.

But would hunters ever have a chance? Trey sure didn't want anyone to suffer the same fate his friends had. How would he ever be able to explain things to their families if he got out of here?

"When," Trey said aloud. When he got out of here. He had to think positively.

He had to find a way out. He had to escape.

The Woodlizards would find him soon. He would have to be prepared.

Trey strained to remember everything that had happened that day. Maybe he had overlooked something that could help him out of this mess. Something that could save him. Leaning his head back against a branch, he shut his eyes, and remembered.

# ARE YOU A

## If so, send us your
### *Cool Drawings*
### or
### SCARY STORIES
## for possible publication in

THE

# N E W S L E T T E R

Send to:
Montage Publications
9808 Waples St.
San Diego, California 92121